TEN LITTLE PRINCESSES

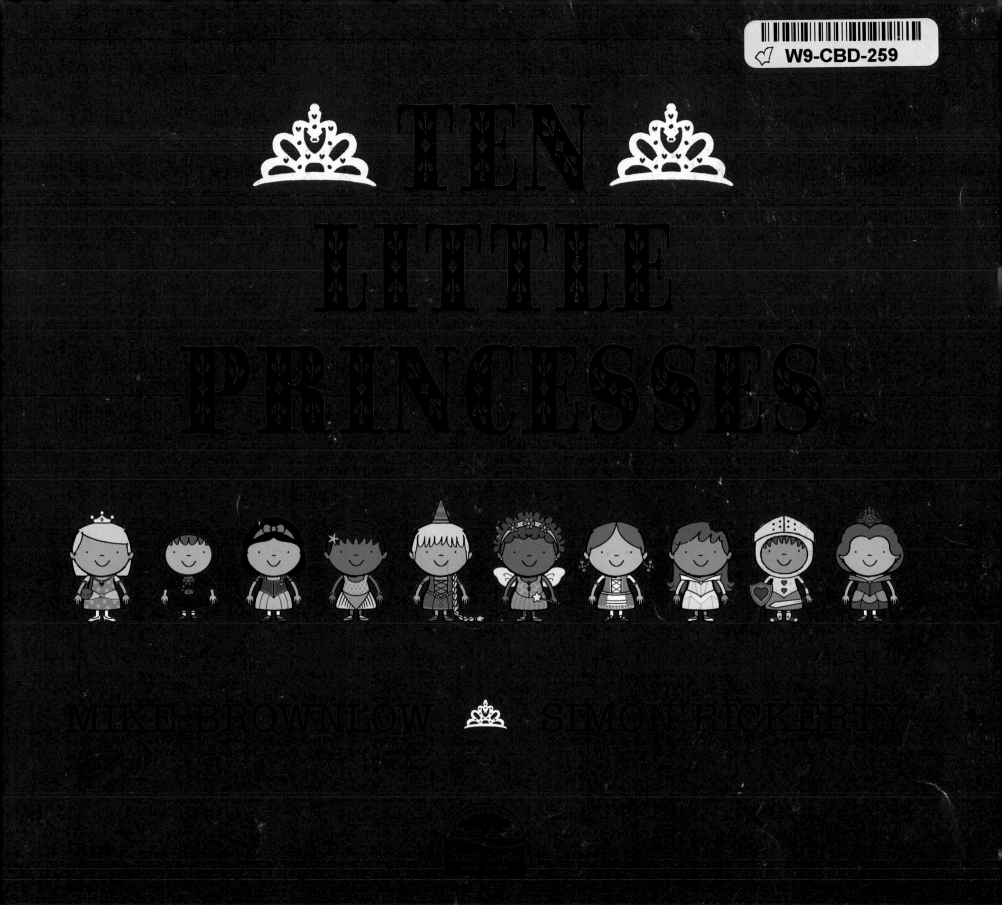

MIKE BROWNLOW · SIMON RICKERTY

Sandy Creek

Ten little princesses, going to the ball,

Trotting on their ponies, past the castle wall.

Are they looking forward to their very special day?

Ten little princesses all shout,

"Yay!"

Ten little princesses, looking quite divine.

"Ouch!"

—a princess pricks her thumb.

10

Now there are . . .

. . . nine.

Nine little princesses,

running rather late.

9

"Crunch!"

goes the poisoned apple.

Now there are . . .

...eight.

Eight little princesses pass a prince who's heaven.

"Hi,"

8

smiles the charming prince.

Now there are . . .

Seven little princesses
hide behind some sticks.

"Huff!"

blows a big bad wolf.

Now there are . . .

Now there are . . . .

...**five.**

5

Five little princesses spot a hairy paw.

"You're a beauty,"

growls the Beast.

Now there are . . .

. . . **four.**

4

**Four little princesses
climb a beanstalk tree.**

"Fee-fi-foe!"

a giant says.

Now there are . . .

...three.

3

Three little princesses don't know what to do.

Whoosh!

roars a dragon's breath.

Now there are . . .

...two.

Two little princesses,
wondering where to run.

2

"Grrrr!"

snarls a sneaky troll.
Now there is . . .

One little princess, feeling sad and blue.

All her friends have disappeared.

Whatever can she do?

The last little princess
makes a special call . . .
She dials her Fairy God Mom
on her magic crystal ball.

Fairy God Mom waves her wand . . .

the others reappear!

The bad guys run, the ball is saved.

It's time to whoop and cheer!

Ten little princesses all shout, "Yay!"

For my own little princesses,
Dilly, Rachel, Sally and Catie
M.B.

For Erin and Isla
S.R.

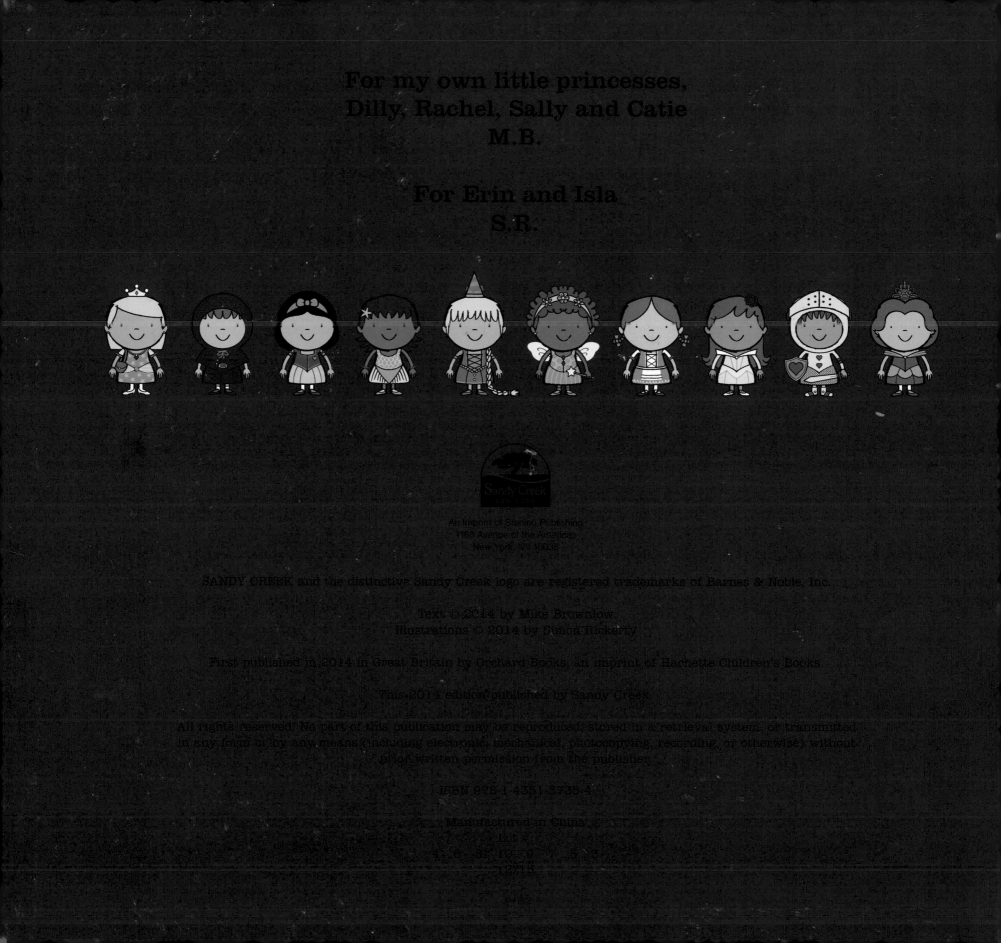

Sandy Creek

An Imprint of Sterling Publishing
1166 Avenue of the Americas
New York, NY 10036

Text © 2014 by Mike Brownlow
Illustrations © 2014 by Simon Rickerty

First published in 2014 in Great Britain by Orchard Books, an imprint of Hachette Children's Books

This 2014 edition published by Sandy Creek

ISBN 978-1-4351-5735-4

Manufactured in China
Lot #
4 6 8 10 9 7 5 3
12/15